Time Goes By

A Year on a
Pirate Ship

Elizabeth Havercroft

M Millbrook Press / Minneapolis

First American edition published in 2009 by Lerner Publishing Group, Inc.

Copyright © 2008 by Orpheus Books Ltd.

Millbrook Press
A division of Lerner Publishing Group, Inc.
241 First Avenue North
Minneapolis, MN 55401 USA

Website address: www.lernerbooks.com

Library of Congress Cataloging-in-Publication Data

Havercroft, Elizabeth.
    A year on a pirate ship / by Elizabeth Havercroft — 1st American ed.
        p.   cm. -- (Time goes by)
    Includes index.
        ISBN 978–1–58013–547–4 (lib. bdg. : alk. paper)
    1. Pirates—Juvenile literature. I. Title.
    G535.H367 2009
    910.4'5—dc22   2007049719

Manufactured in the United States of America
1 2 3 4 5 6 — BP — 14 13 12 11 10 09

Table of Contents

THIS IS THE STORY of what takes place during a year on a pirate ship. Each picture shows the pirates' adventures as the months go by. Lots of things happen, even far out at sea. Can you spot them all?

Some pictures have parts of the ship's walls taken away. This helps you see what's going on below deck. You can follow all the exciting action as the weeks pass. The calendar on each right-hand page tells you which month you've reached.

Lots of work goes into running a ship—as well as attacking other ships! The pirates find some of the work boring. But they enjoy plenty of excitement too. The captain and first mate make sure the crew is ready for anything that happens.

Some characters appear in every picture. Look out for a clumsy pirate. Another pirate sleeps through all the action. Did you spot the women pirates? Don't miss the monkey and the turtle who travel along with the pirate ship!

Can you find . . .

a barrel?

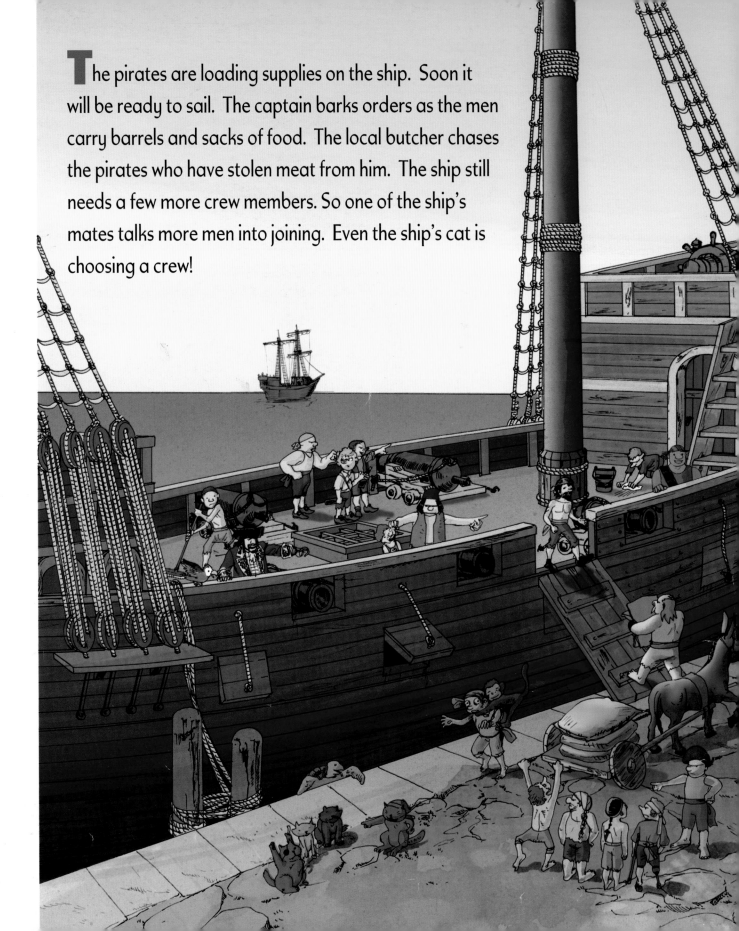

The pirates are loading supplies on the ship. Soon it will be ready to sail. The captain barks orders as the men carry barrels and sacks of food. The local butcher chases the pirates who have stolen meat from him. The ship still needs a few more crew members. So one of the ship's mates talks more men into joining. Even the ship's cat is choosing a crew!

January

Loading the ship

Setting sail

Stuck in weeds

Pirate attack!

Island life

Whale watching

A huge storm

Shipwrecked

a dolphin?

the chef?

The ship is in full sail. This means all the sails are fully spread out. The pirates don't fly their flag, the Jolly Roger. They do so only when they attack a ship. Way up in the crow's nest, a crew member is on the lookout for ships to rob. Some pirates scrub the deck. Others mend sails. The captain checks the map. Below deck, one pirate feeds the pigs. Another helps himself to food supplies.

Loading the ship

Setting sail

Stuck in weeds

Pirate attack!

Island life

Whale watching

A huge storm

Shipwrecked

Can you find . . .

a man
throwing knives?

men
scrubbing the deck?

the first mate?

The day is hot, with no wind. The ship can't use its sails. Worse still, the ship gets stuck in floating weeds. The captain loses his temper with the ship's navigator. Getting stuck is all his fault! Some pirates try to keep busy. But most of them are bored. One pirate catches a surprise while fishing.

April

Loading the ship

Setting sail

Stuck in weeds

Pirate attack!

Island life

Whale watching

A huge storm

Shipwrecked

a cutlass?

a woman pirate?

an anchor?

a cannon?

At last, the pirates have found a merchant ship to attack. It's likely to carry treasure from selling its goods. The pirates raise the Jolly Roger. Guns blazing, they sail close to the merchant ship. When they're close enough, they throw wooden planks between the two ships. Pirates rush across the planks with their weapons ready. Some pirates swing to the merchant ship using ropes. Even the parrot and monkey join the action. The fighting is fierce. A shot whistles straight through the captain's hat.

May

Loading the ship

Setting sail

Stuck in weeds

Pirate attack!

Island life

Whale watching

A huge storm

Shipwrecked

Can you
find . . .

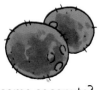

a sandcastle?

some coconuts?

the captured captain?

a fish bone?

The pirates overpower the merchant ship and capture its crew. The pirates help themselves to the ship's supplies. Then they let the ship float out to sea. The pirates anchor their own ship off a nearby island. They row the captured captain and his crew ashore. The merchant crew will be stuck there. While on the island, the pirates dig for buried treasure. Some pirates even have time to sunbathe, picnic, and build sandcastles!

June

Loading the ship

Setting sail

Stuck in weeds

Pirate attack!

Island life

Whale watching

A huge storm

Shipwrecked

Can you find . . .

an accordion?

the ship's navigator?

a seagull?

a turtle?

the pirate captain?

The pirate ship is back at sea. The pirates are in a joyful mood. They sing and dance to the music of an accordion. The captured treasure will make them rich. They also have enough supplies to last for a long time. Without warning, a whale swims next to the ship. Its blowhole opens wide. It sprays the ship with water. The pirates try to scare away the whale.

September

Loading the ship

Setting sail

Stuck in weeds

Pirate attack!

Island life

Whale watching

A huge storm

Shipwrecked

Can you
find . . .

an ax?

a pirate hanging on?

an oar?

the ship's wheel?

A huge storm brews. Rain beats down on the ship. Giant waves try to turn it over. Some of the crew try to control the wheel. Suddenly, lightning strikes the ship's mast, or main pole. The mast snaps in two. The ship starts sinking. The pirates try to stay out of the sea. Meanwhile, the cowardly captain stays below deck to guard his treasure.

Loading the ship

Setting sail

Stuck in weeds

Pirate attack!

Island life

Whale watching

A huge storm

Shipwrecked

the Jolly Roger?

a telescope?

an octopus?

a pelican?

The storm went on for a long time. Waves crashed over the ship's sides. They tore it apart. Luckily, the sea was not too deep. Some pirates are holding on to the ship's stern, or back end. It is sticking out of the water. Others cling to floating pieces of wood. They have been shipwrecked for weeks. They are hungry, thirsty, and bored. Worse, sharks are everywhere. Suddenly, someone spots a ship. The pirates do all they can to get its crew's attention. They shout, wave, and light a fire. Will the ship pick them up?

Glossary

accordion: a musical instrument that is squeezed to make sound

blowhole: the hole in a whale's head out of which it sprays water

crow's nest: a small platform at the top of the mast, from which a sailor can see far away

cutlass: a short, curved sword

first mate: the officer who is second in command on a ship

full sail: having all sails raised and fully open

goods: things to sell

Jolly Roger: the black flag used by pirates. It usually shows a skull and crossed bones.

mast: the tall main pole that supports a ship's sails

mates: a ship's officers

merchant ship: a ship that carries goods to trade

navigator: a person who guides a ship, using maps, the stars, and tools such as compasses

pelican: a large seabird

stern: the back end of a ship

Learn More about Pirates

Books

Helbrough, Emma. *A Day in the Life of a Pirate.* New York: PowerKids Press, 2007.

Jarman, Julia. *Class Three at Sea.* Minneapolis: Carolrhoda Books, 2008.

Long, Melinda. *How I Became a Pirate.* San Diego: Harcourt, 2003.

Steele, Philip. *The Amazing World of Pirates.* London: Southwater, 2008.

Teitelbaum, Michael. *Pirate Life.* Chanhassen, MN: Child's World, 2007.

Yolen, Jane. *The Ballad of the Pirate Queens.* San Diego: Harcourt, 1995.

Websites

A to Z Kid's Stuff

http://www.atozkidstuff.com/pirates.html

This site has quizzes, pages to color, and pirate stuff to make.

National Geographic Pirate Site

http://www.nationalgeographic.com/pirates

This site has mysteries to solve and treasure to find!

A Closer Look

This book has a lot to find. Did you see people who showed up again and again? Think about what these people did and saw during the year. If these people kept journals, what would they write? A journal is a book with blank pages where people write down their thoughts. Have you ever kept a journal? What did you write about?

Try making a journal for one of the characters in this book. You will need a pencil and a piece of paper. Choose your character. Give your character a name. Write the name of the month at the top of the page. Underneath, write about the character's life during that month. Pretend you are the character. What kind of work are you doing? Is your work hard or easy? Is it exciting or boring? Why? What is your life like on the pirate ship? Have you seen anything surprising? What?

Don't worry if you don't know how to spell every word. You can ask a parent or teacher for help if you need to. And be creative!

Index